Ellie Bean the Drama Queen

by Jennie Harding

illustrated by David Padgett

FUTURE HORIZONS INC.

Ellie Bean the Drama Queen

All marketing and publishing rights guaranteed to and reserved by:

FUTURE HORIZONS INC.

721 W. Abram St, Arlington, TX 76013
Phone 800•489•0727
Fax 817•277•2270
www.FHautism.com

ISBN 13: 978-1-935567-27-1

This book is dedicated to my husband, Scott, for pushing me every day
to follow through with my ideas, as crazy as they may seem.

To my son Colin, for his creativity and imagination,
and for encouraging me to open my mind and think big.

Finally, to my daughter, Ellie, whose spirit and spunk,
despite her struggles, inspire me to believe in myself
and be proud of my accomplishments.

With her unevenly cut brown hair, bare feet, and loud, munchkin-like singing voice, Ellie Bean spun wildly in circles in her backyard.

As the wind blew harder against her face, Ellie Bean laughed and sang louder…

and louder!

and louder…

Her spinning became faster…

and faster!

"Slow down, Bean!" her mother yelled from the house.

Ellie stopped suddenly. The multiple rotations she made while spinning made her giddy with delight, but she never ever appeared wobbly.

In fact, she instantly took off running after a passing butterfly.

Just as the butterfly fluttered through the air, so did Ellie Bean's attention.

She would soon focus her interest elsewhere...

"AAHH! Oh no! A bee! A bee!!!"

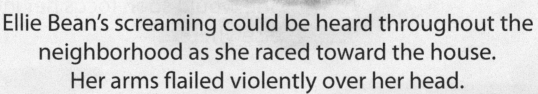

Ellie Bean's screaming could be heard throughout the
neighborhood as she raced toward the house.
Her arms flailed violently over her head.

As her mom opened up the back door, Ellie ran full-force right into her arms. Ellie's mom gave her a big bear hug.

In a quiet and very reassuring voice, she asked, "Okay, Ellie Bean —now what happened?"

Unfortunately, Ellie was unable to put her fear into words. Even more upsetting for both Ellie and her mother, this was not the first time Ellie had a hard time telling her mom what was wrong.

In fact, there were many things that upset Ellie—things that made Ellie feel…just not quite right. And when Ellie did not feel right, everyone knew what would happen! She would cry. She would scream. She would run around frantically, and it seemed like she could not stop.

Some people thought Ellie didn't want to stop. Some people thought that she was being a brat. Some people thought that she liked to cry and scream.

Some people thought that Ellie Bean was a "*drama queen.*"

Only Ellie knew that the reason why she cried for so long was that the tag on her shirt felt like it was digging into her back.

Only Ellie knew that the reason why she screamed so loudly was that brushing her teeth felt awful. The bristles on the toothbrush felt like they were scratching her teeth, and the smell and taste of the toothpaste made her stomach do somersaults!

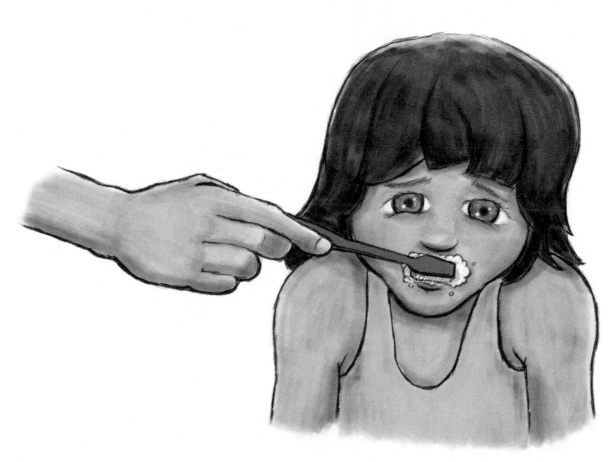

The flush of the toilet…TOO LOUD!

Getting her hair cut…OUCH!

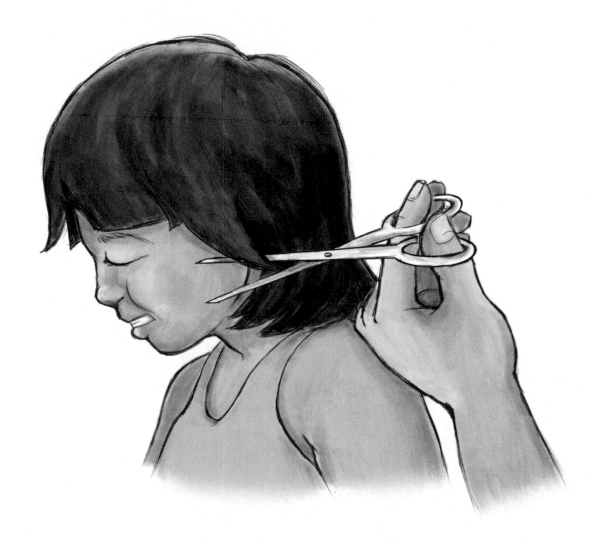

Ellie found that every day, there was something that was too loud, too scratchy, too painful, too tight, too smelly, or too squishy.

Ellie Bean's mom wanted her to feel good. She wanted to help Ellie to tell people what was wrong. So, Ellie's mom took her to see a special person.

That special person was called an occupational therapist.
Her name was Miss Gail.

Ellie would swing on her special swing…

and she would jump on a mini-trampoline.

Ellie also liked it when Miss Gail used a special brush to brush her arms and legs.

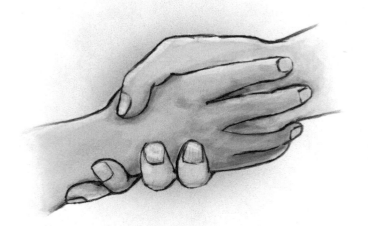

Then Miss Gail squeezed Ellie Bean's arms and hands.

All of this made Ellie feel much better.

Miss Gail worked and played with Ellie. She found out that Ellie felt better after she spent time on a special swing. She also found out that there were many activities and exercises that made Ellie feel better.

Miss Gail showed Ellie Bean's mom all of the activities that helped Ellie feel calm. The more Ellie and her mom did these exercises, the better she felt.

And as Ellie began to feel better… the screaming was not as loud. The crying did not go on and on and on.

And soon, Ellie Bean began to use words to tell her mom all about the things that were…

As she began to feel better and talk more…

Ellie's mom, Miss Gail, and many other people who loved Ellie could help her more and more.

Soon, other people started to see that Ellie Bean really wasn't a *drama queen.*

BUT...
She did keep the crown!

What Is Sensory Processing Disorder?

An important point to remember about Sensory Processing Disorder (SPD) is that it is a term used to cover an array of neurological disabilities—not just one. SPD is an umbrella term used to describe the inability to use information received from the senses to function smoothly in daily life.[1] There are three categories of SPD. As described in the book *The Out-of-Sync Child*, by Carol Stock Kranowitz, these three categories include five subtypes, all of which occur within the central nervous system. The inability to process information that the brain receives has a negative effect on the way a child organizes, plans, and behaves. Ultimately, this inability has a negative impact on learning.

SPD in School: My Experience as a Special Educator

As a special educator, many of the children I work with struggle to process a variety of sensory messages throughout their school day. There are many classroom strategies that you can utilize as a teacher to support a child with a SPD.

It is important to recognize your own understanding of SPD. It is extremely important to educate yourself to be able to better assist students in your classroom. An understanding of the signs and symptoms of SPD will help you to identify and document potential sensory red flags. More importantly, seek out related service professionals in your building. An occupational therapist will not only be able to assist you with information that is useful for your own understanding but will also be able to aid in your facilitation of sensory interventions.

SPD at Home: My Experience as a Parent

As a parent of a child with sensory-processing difficulties, I find myself agreeing wholeheartedly with the hopes described in Lucy Jane Miller's book, *Sensational Kids*.[2] My hopes for Ellie are that she is accepted socially by her peers and, with that acceptance, she will have the strength and confidence to participate in anything that is of interest to her. I also hope that she becomes more aware of her sensory needs and, with that awareness, that she becomes better able to express her wants and needs. In addition to my hopes for Ellie, I also want to continue to educate myself and others about strategies that are helpful when interacting with Ellie.

As stated in the previous section, the most important strategy in helping your child with SPD at home is to educate yourself and seek the assistance of professionals in the field. Occupational therapists available through the school system and those who provide private therapy can offer you information and support groups to assist you in learning more about SPD. In addition, occupational therapists can also assist in the creation of a sensory diet that can be implemented at home. A sensory diet is a planned and scheduled program that an occupational therapist develops to help a person become more self-regulated.

References

1. Kranowitz CS. *The Out-of-Sync Child*. New York, NY: Penguin Books; 2005.
2. Miller LJ. *Sensational Kids*. New York, NY: G.P. Putnam's Sons; 2006.

Special Thanks

A special thank-you to my daughter, Ellie "Bean" Harding—I love you dearly. You teach me more and more every day.

Also, thank you to Gail Masse, occupational therapist and colleague. You gave me so much advice, information, and—most importantly—support.

About the Author

Jennie Harding and her husband, Scott, live in Maumee, Ohio, along with their two children—Colin and Ellie. Jennie has taught for 14 years and has her bachelor's and master's degrees in moderate-to-intense special education. Ellie, now age 7, has been receiving occupational therapy for sensory-processing difficulties since the age of 4. Jennie's desire to educate herself and help Ellie and others with this disorder was her purpose for writing this book. Jennie's passion for teaching and love for her daughter motivated her to become an SPD parent-connections host. She hopes to offer support and knowledge to other parents to better help their own children with special needs.

About the Illustrator

A native of Cincinnati, David Padgett has been drawing his entire life. After earning a bachelor's degree in graphic design and painting at Miami University in Ohio, David worked as a graphic designer in Cincinnati and Chicago. He is currently employed as a digital artist and freelance illustrator in Toledo, Ohio, where he lives with his wife, Brooke, and his dog, Brody. He is inspired by great design, midcentury modern architecture, and superheroes.

Resources
Web Sites

The Sensory Processing Disorder Foundation, *www.spdfoundation.net/*
The Sensory and Motor Integration Web site of the University of Texas at Austin, *www.edb.utexas.edu/utap/smi/*
The Sensory Integration Global Network, *www.siglobalnetwork.org/*

Books

Tools for Tots, by Diana A. Henry, Maureen Kane-Wineland, and Susan Swindeman (2007)
The Out-of-Sync Child, by Carol Stock Kranowitz (2005)
Sensational Kids, by Lucy Jane Miller (2006)

Additional Resources

Sensory World, a proud imprint of Sensory Focus, LLC, is the world's largest publisher devoted exclusively to resources for those interested in Sensory Processing Disorder. They also sponsor national conferences for parents, teachers, therapists, and others interested in supporting those with Sensory Processing Disorder. Visit *www.sensoryworld.com* for further information.

Sensory World
Jennifer Gilpin Yacio, President
888•507•2193 (phone and fax)
info@sensoryworld.com (email)
www.sensoryworld.com

Additional Resources

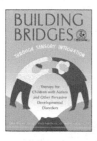

Paula Aquilla, Ellen Yack, & Shirley Sutton
Building Bridges through Sensory Integration, 2nd ed.
www.sensoryworld.com

Bonnie Arnwine
Starting Sensory Therapy:
Fun Activities for Your Home or Classroom!
www.fhautism.com

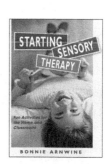

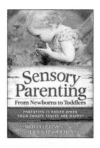

Britt Collins & Jackie Olson
Sensory Parenting: From Newborns to Toddlers Everything
Is Easier When Your Child's Senses Are Happy!
www.fhautism.com

Marla S. Fisch
Sensitive Sam: A Sensitive Story with a
Happy Ending for Parents and Kids!
www.fhautism.com

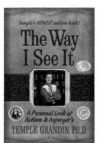

Temple Grandin
The Way I See It and *Thinking in Pictures*
www.fhautism.com

Carol Gray
The New Social Story Book
www.fhautism.com

David Jereb & Kathy Koehler Jereb
 MoveAbout Activity Cards: Quick and Easy Sensory Activities to Help Children Refocus, Calm Down or Regain Energy
www.fhautism.com

Joan Krzyzanowski, Patricia Angermeier, & Kristina Keller Moir
Learning in Motion: 101+ Fun Classroom Activities
www.fhautism.com

Jane Koomar, Stacey Szklut, Carol Kranowitz, et al
Answers to Questions Teachers Ask About Sensory Integration
www.sensoryworld.com

Aubrey Lande & Bob Wiz
Songames™ for Sensory Integration (CD)
www.sensoryworld.com

Rebecca Moyes
Building Sensory Friendly Classrooms to Support Children with Challenging Behaviors
www.sensoryworld.com

Laurie Renke, Jake Renke, & Max Renke
I Like Birthdays…It's the Parties I'm Not Sure About!
www.fhautism.com

John Taylor
Learn to Have Fun with Your Senses!
The Sensory Avoider's Survival Guide
www.fhautism.com

Kelly Tilley
Active Imagination Activity Book:
50 Sensorimotor Activities to Improve
Focus, Attention, Strength, & Coordination
www.fhautism.com

Carol Kranowitz
The Out-of-Sync Child, 2nd ed; *The Out-of-Sync Child Has Fun*, 2nd ed; Getting Kids in Sync (DVD featuring the children of St. Columba's Nursery School); *Growing an In-Sync Child*; Sensory Issues in Learning & Behavior (DVD); *The Goodenoughs Get in Sync*; *Preschool Sensory Scan for Educators* (Preschool SENSE) Manual and Forms Packet
www.sensoryworld.com

These catalog companies can provide more ideas
and products for kids with special needs.

School Speciality
(888) 388-3224
www.schoolspecialtyonline.net

FlagHouse Sensory Solution
(800) 793-7900
www.FlagHouse.com

Henry Occupational Therapy Services, Inc.
(623) 882-8812
www.ateachabout.com

Therapro, Inc.
(800) 257-5376
www.theraproducts.com